Dear mouse friends,
Welcome to the world of

Geronimo Stilton

THE RODENT'S GAZETTE
EDITORIAL STAFF

Geronimo Stilton
A learned and brainy
mouse; editor of
The Rodent's Gazette

Thea Stilton
Geronimo's sister and
special correspondent at
The Rodent's Gazette

Trap Stilton
An awful joker;
Geronimo's cousin and
owner of the store
Cheap Junk for Less

Benjamin Stilton
A sweet and loving
nine-year-old mouse;
Geronimo's favorite
nephew

Geronimo Stilton

OPERATION: SECRET RECIPE

Scholastic Inc.

Published by Scholastic Inc., *Publishers since 1920,* 557 Broadway, New York, NY 10012. SCHOLASTIC and associated logos are trademarks and/or registered trademarks of Scholastic Inc.

Stilton is the name of a famous English cheese. It is a registered trademark of the Stilton Cheese Makers' Association. For more information, go to www.stiltoncheese.com.

ISBN 978-1-338-08782-6

Text by Geronimo Stilton
Original title *Operazione panettone*
Cover by Roberto Ronchi (design) and Andrea Cavallini (color)
Illustrations by Danilo Loizedda (design), Valeria Cairoli (pencils and inks), and Daria Cerchi and Serena Gianoli (color)
Graphics by Michela Battaglin

Special thanks to Shannon Penney
Translated by Julia Heim
Interior design by Kevin Callahan/BNGO Books

10 9 8 7 6 5 4 3 2 1   17 18 19 20 21

Printed in the U.S.A.   40
First printing 2017

SNORE, SNORE, SNORE . . . SQUEAK?

One calm spring *morning*, I was home in my mousehole SNORING AWAY in my comfy little bed . . .

Zzzzzzzzzz . . .

Well, I was snoozing peacefully until **suddenly** someone started throwing rocks at my bedroom window!

Bang, bang, bang, bang, bang, bang, bang, bang!

I checked the time. Holey cheese — it was five o'clock in the morning!

I rolled over and closed my eyes, muttering,

"Slimy Swiss balls, go away — I'm sleepy!"

Then someone rang the buzzer.

Bzzzzz-bz-bzzz-bzzz-bzzz...BZZZZZZZZZZ!

Slimy Swiss balls, go away!

Who could it be?

I put the pillow over my head and **GRUMBLED**, "Some of us are in the middle of very important sleeping!"

But a moment later, I heard a knock on my door.

Knock, knock, knock, knock, knock, knock, knock!

At the same time, my home phone started ringing. I was getting all kinds of text messages and emails on my cell phone, too!

Ring ring riiiiing!

Bing! Bing! Bing!

Putrid cheese puffs, that's enough!

Ding! Ding! Ding!

Ding! Ding! Ding!

I **ROLLED** out of bed, yelling at the top of my lungs, "Putrid cheese puffs, that's enough! I want to sleep!"

Just then, someone shouted,

"Geronimooooo!"

I couldn't tell who in the world was squeaking. This wasn't just one voice—it was a whole chorus of different voices! Even so, they sounded familiar . . .

THUNDERING CATTAILS!

Sighing, I trudged out my front door—and could hardly believe my eyes! Parked in front of my house was an ultra-modern **Super RV**.

You may think I'm squeaking nonsense, dear rodent friends, but I swear that this RV . . .

. . . was as long as a train car!

 . . . was as wide as a truck!

. . . and was as tall as a three-story house!

Basically, the cheese-colored Super RV was completely **ENORMOUSE**!

And that's not all! Most of my family and **friends** were poking their snouts out of the RV's windows. **THOSE** were the voices I'd heard!

The Stilton Family Super RV

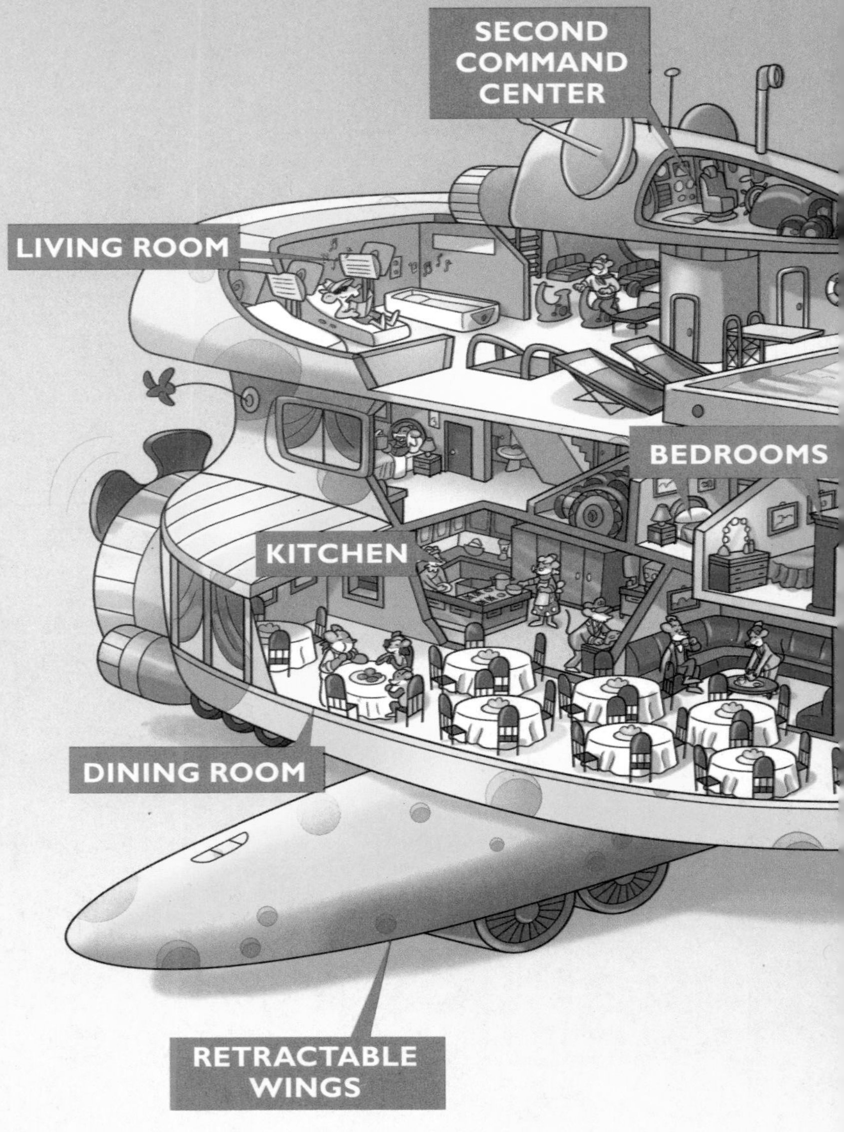

SECOND COMMAND CENTER

LIVING ROOM

BEDROOMS

KITCHEN

DINING ROOM

RETRACTABLE WINGS

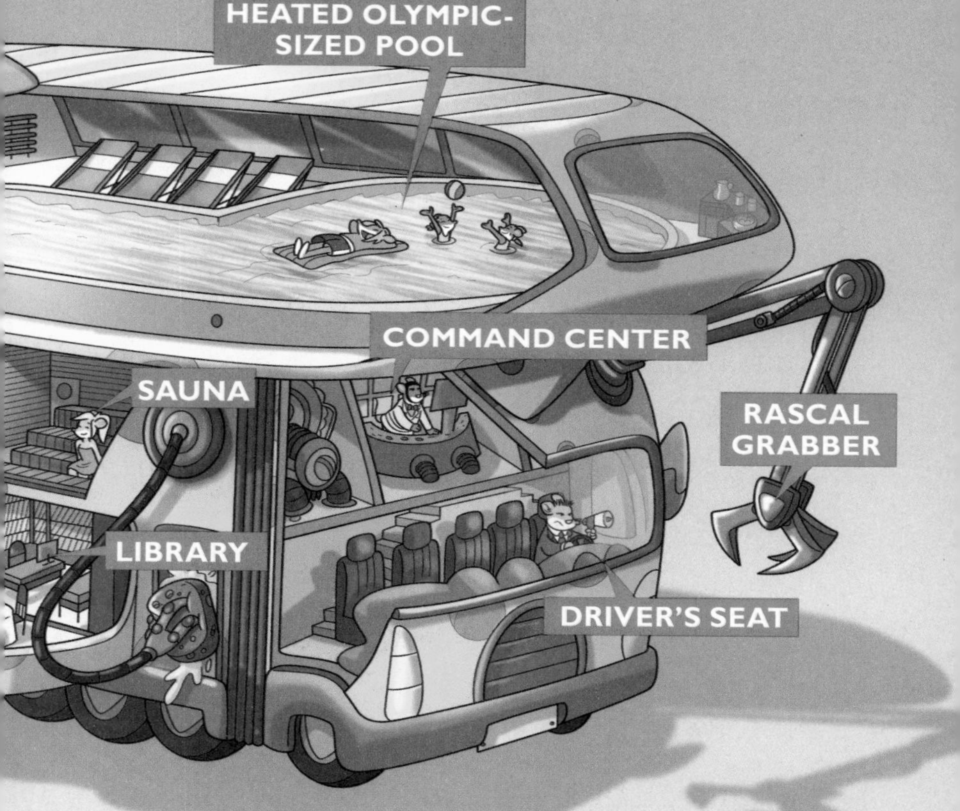

HEATED OLYMPIC-SIZED POOL

COMMAND CENTER

SAUNA

RASCAL GRABBER

LIBRARY

DRIVER'S SEAT

Super RV

This is an RV unlike any other — it transforms into all different fabumouse vehicles! It can drive on the street like a car, fly in the sky like a plane, or sail the seas like a boat.

But I'm in My Pajamas!

Rubbing my eyes, I ran toward the Super RV. As soon as I approached, a door suddenly popped open: *Pop!*

. . . A claw came out: *Zip!*

. . . It grabbed me by my pajama shirt: *Zap!*

. . . And it ripped off three buttons: *Riiip!*

I began to thrash around. Was this thing ever going to put me down?

"SQUEEEEAAAKKK!"

Grandfather William leaned out of the Super RV and thundered through a megaphone, "Grandson, we need to leave **right away**!"

"What? **Leave?**" I stammered. "But I

can't leave—I'm in my *pajamas*!"

My sister Thea hollered, "No excuses, Geronimo! I brought you some clothes. Anything else you need, you can buy in Milan!"

"Moldy mozzarella!" I cried. "Milan? You mean, the city in Italy? Why would I go to Milan?"

My cousin TRAP rolled his eyes. "I told you he would try to play dumb! *I knew he wouldn't want to come to Milan.*"

Moldy mozzarella!

We need to leave right away!

My friend Hercule Poirat leaned out of one of the RV's windows. "Oh, Geronimo, don't be a CHEDDARHEAD! Let's go!"

Bruce Hyena added, "Get moving! Milan is waiting!"

"Stilton, do you want to lie around eating cheese all day, or do you want to come on a fabumouse adventure?" Grandfather's friend Professor Cheesepuff asked. He had invented the Super RV with his own two paws!

Mmmm . . . eating cheese all day sounded pretty good to me . . .

I shook my snout. "At least tell me why I should go to Milan with you."

TRAP held up his paws before anyone else could squeak. "Leave

Why Milan?

this to me!" He grinned and pushed a button.

Before I knew what was happening, a steel net surrounded me and pulled me inside the Super RV. **SQUEAK!**

Crusty cat litter! I was on my way to Milan . . . *but why*?

As soon as I was inside the Super RV, all my friends and family pulled off the steel net and ***hugged*** me.

It was hard to keep my tail in a twist surrounded by so much love! I hugged them all back and said, "Well, thanks for inviting me . . . I mean, *capturing* me! Even though I have a million other things to do, I guess I'll come with you to Milan!"

i love you all, too!

HAVE YOU WRITTEN YOUR WILL?

Grandfather handed off the Super RV's controls to Thea. Grinning, she yelled, **"Hold on to your fur, everymouse!"**

I had barely managed to buckle my seat belt when the Super RV's engine **ROARED** noisily.

"MILAN, HERE WE COME!" Thea cried.

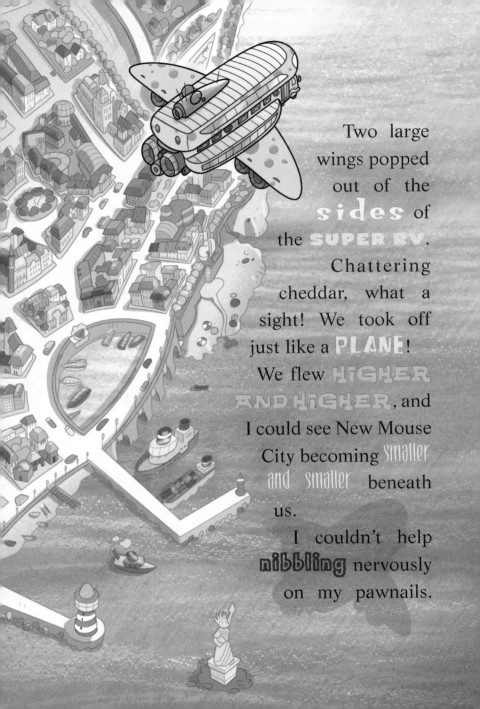

Two large wings popped out of the **sides** of the **SUPER RV**. Chattering cheddar, what a sight! We took off just like a **PLANE**! We flew **HIGHER AND HIGHER**, and I could see New Mouse City becoming **smaller and smaller** beneath us.

I couldn't help **nibbling** nervously on my pawnails.

"Excuse me, Professor Cheesepuff? Are you absolutely sure that it's not dangerous to fly in the Super RV?"

Are you trying to say that isn't safe?

Professor Cheesepuff frowned. OOPS, had I offended him? "Stilton, are you trying to say that the Super RV isn't safe?"

Just then, Trap grabbed my paw. "Oh, Geronimo, look how that wing is SHAKING! And look there, a BOLT has fallen off! Holey cheese balls, I may have forgotten to fill the tank with gas!" He yelled, "HEEEEELP! We're fallllliiiinnnggggggg! Geronimo, have you written your will? Remember to leave me your cheese rind collection from the seventeen hundreds!"

Rat-munching rattlesnakes!

Help!

Ha, ha, ha!

Thundering cattails!

It was just a joke!

"Heeeellllppppp!"

I squeaked at the top of my lungs.

But then I realized that Trap was **SNICKERING** and winking at Thea. My sister turned around and **shook** her snout. "Oh, Geronimo, it was just a *joke*..."

I turned *red* from the ends of my ears to the tip of my tail! I should have known!

Professor Cheesepuff stared sharply at me over his **GLASSES**. "Stilton, have you at least studied up on Milan? When was the city founded? How **big** is it? How many rodents live there?"

"Well, actually, I didn't study at all! I didn't know that we would be going to Milan until sunrise."

The professor Rolled his eyes. "Well, Stilton, you failed your first test of the trip. Get it together, cheesebrain!"

Have you studied?

Then he quizzed Benjamin and BUGSY, who answered every question in unison.

Professor Cheesepuff nodded, satisfied. "FABUMOUSE—unlike that uncle of yours! I give you both a hundred percent!"

Then he pressed a button, and the Super RV's screen began to play a *3-D film* about the history of Milan.

ORIGINS OF THE CITY'S NAME

According to legend, the name "Milan" is derived from the Latin phrase *In Medio Lanae*, which means "half covered in wool," like the boar sow carved on an ancient stone that was found in Milan long ago. But there are other theories behind the name! For instance, the ancient Latin name *Mediolanum* means "Middle Land," and could refer to the city's geographical location.

THE HISTORY OF MILAN

Milan was one of the capitals of the Western Roman Empire. In the Middle Ages it was a Commune, then a city-state under the Visconti and Sforza families. Milan was later governed by France, Spain, and Austria at different times, and then played a significant role in the period leading up to *Risorgimento*—Italy's unification. Since 1861, it has been part of Italy.

MILAN TODAY

Today, you can find almost anything in Milan — skyscrapers that tower above the city, ancient palaces with secret courtyards, museums, libraries, beautiful gardens and parks . . . and really fabumouse pastry shops!

MILANESE CUISINE

Milan's traditional dishes include yellow saffron risotto, Milanese veal cutlets, *cassoeula* (a stew made with cabbage and pork), *mondeghili* (meatballs), and the legendary *panettone* (Christmas cake)!

WELCOME TO MILAN!

After hours and hours of flying, we finally arrived in Milan. I could see a long canal below us.

"Hang on to your whiskers—we're about to land!" Thea called.

The **Super RV** slowly descended and landed on the water.

Splash!
Splash! Splash!
Splash! Splash!

Then Thea pressed another button. Wheels popped out of the Super RV, and we suddenly rolled up onto the street. Cheesy cream puffs, this vehicle was full of **surprises**!

THE *NAVIGLI*

The marble that was used to build the famouse Duomo di Milano (Milan's cathedral) arrived on large ships, which sailed directly into the city on canals! This network of canals throughout Milan was called the *Navigli*. Centuries later, most of the canals were filled in and covered. Today, cars drive on roads where there used to be water!

As we rolled along the street, the Super RV shook like a **wet** dog:

Brrrrzzzzooottttt!

Then it let out a bunch of **hot air** to dry itself off:

WHOOOOOOSH!

WHOOOOOOSH!

WHOOOOOOSH!

Next, some MECHANICAL hands began to frantically polish the Super RV with rags and wax.

SWISH! SWWWWISSSHHH! SWISH!

Finally, we continued along roads PACKED with cars, until we arrived in the heart of Milan. Holey cheese, I could hardly contain my squeaks of excitement!

Sticking my snout out the window, I could see pink marble *towers* and a golden statue sparkling in the sun.

It was the Duomo di Milano — the famouse Milan Cathedral!

THE MILAN CATHEDRAL
(DUOMO DI MILANO)

This marvemouse cathedral took centuries to complete—and it's being restored to this day! As a result, the people of Milan have been known to use the expression "It's like building the cathedral" to describe a job that seems endless. The Duomo is home to 3,400 statues. More than half of the statues are outside, and many can be seen from the cathedral's roof. The view from the top of the Duomo is truly fabumouse!

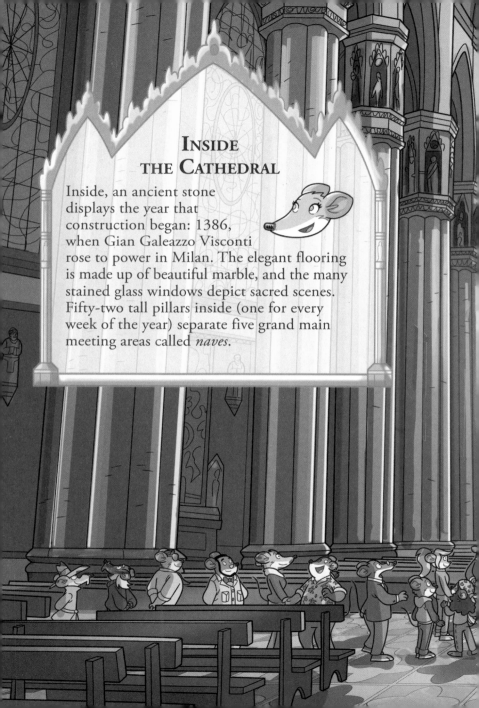

INSIDE THE CATHEDRAL

Inside, an ancient stone displays the year that construction began: 1386, when Gian Galeazzo Visconti rose to power in Milan. The elegant flooring is made up of beautiful marble, and the many stained glass windows depict sacred scenes. Fifty-two tall pillars inside (one for every week of the year) separate five grand main meeting areas called *naves*.

WHAT A HIKE!

As we walked out of the **DUOMO**, Grandfather William held up his **megaphone** and thundered, "**LISTEN UP**, crew, it's time to get moving—we're climbing to the top of the **cathedral**!"

Cheese and crackers, that sounded like a lot of work! "Does someone want to explain why we came to **Milan**?" I squeaked. "And why do we have to climb the cathedral?"

You're not thinking of spending money, are you?

Grandfather's only response was, "Quit squeaking and climb, Grandson! You'll **FIND OUT** when we're at the top!"

With a shrug, I headed toward the **elevator**, but my uncle Samuel Stingysnout grabbed me by the 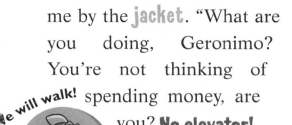jacket. "What are you doing, Geronimo? You're not thinking of **We will walk!** spending money, are you? **No elevator!** The ticket costs less if you take the stairs!"

Bruce Hyena jumped in. "Come on, you big ball of cheese mush, the climb to the top is nothing!"

I began to climb . . . and climb . . . and climb . . . more than two hundred steps!

Puff! Pant!

Come on, you big ball of cheese mush!

THE CATHEDRAL CLIMB

The terraces of the Duomo look out over the cathedral's adornments, flying buttresses, and carved figures. From there, visitors have a fabumouse view of the entire city!

Holey cheese, even my tail was tired!

But when I reached the top, my complaints VANISHED like a cheese platter at a rat's birthday party. What a marvemouse sight!

As we admired the city from above, I asked again, "Now can someone explain why we came to Milan?"

Behind me, a voice squeaked up politely. "You must be Geronimo Stilton! I can explain everything . . ."

I turned and saw a young rodent with a kind expression on his snout.

Thea hugged him. "Hi, Scooter! It's fabumouse to see you!"

The mouse hugged Thea, then shook my paw politely. "Welcome to Milan! I'm SCOOTER BOOKWORM. Today, I'm going to show you a precious treasure that no other rodent has ever seen before. And tomorrow, I'll be presenting it to press from all over the world!"

Grandfather William pinched my ear. "This will be a **MOUSETASTIC SCOOP** for *The Rodent's Gazette*. Now do you **UNDERSTAND** why we've come to Milan, Grandson? Or do I have to spell everything out for you?"

Nice to meet you!

Welcome to Milan!

SCOOTER BOOKWORM

Even though he's very young, Scooter Bookworm is already a history professor, specializing in the history of Milan! He loves books, especially antique ones, and he has an enormouse collection of them. He's also a huge fan of motorcycles, just like Thea — that's why they've been friends for such a long time!

PANETTONE FOR EVERYONE!

SCOOTER led us to the entrance of the Royal Palace, which was right next to the Duomo. **EYES** sparkling with excitement, he announced, "Tomorrow morning at ten o'clock sharp, **The History of Milan** exhibit is set to open. Journalists and television crews from all over the world will be here! I'm planning to present an ancient **scroll** that shows the original secret recipe for panettone, the Christmas cake that has become Milan's most famouse dessert. Plus, we'll have **free** samples of panettone for everyone!"

Yum!

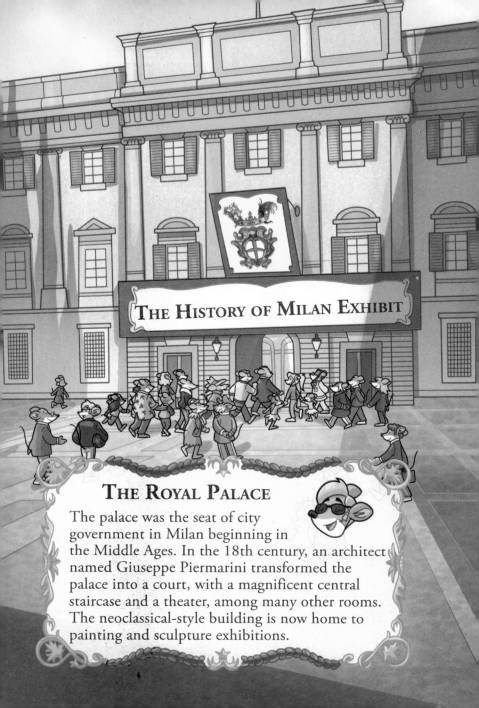

THE HISTORY OF MILAN EXHIBIT

THE ROYAL PALACE

The palace was the seat of city government in Milan beginning in the Middle Ages. In the 18th century, an architect named Giuseppe Piermarini transformed the palace into a court, with a magnificent central staircase and a theater, among many other rooms. The neoclassical-style building is now home to painting and sculpture exhibitions.

Trap licked his whiskers. "Free samples? **Yum!**"

Scooter smiled. "Follow me—I'll give you a sneak peek at the secret recipe!"

But as soon as he entered the palace's famous Hall of Caryatids, Scooter's fur turned as WHITE as mozzarella, and he squeaked in disbelief. "Slimy Swiss balls, someone STOLE the scroll with the original panettone recipe!"

Holey cheese, what a disaster!

THE HISTORY OF PANETTONE

In the 15th century, one of Milanese Duke Ludovico Sforza's cooks accidentally burned a dessert in the oven! He needed to come up with a replacement fast, so he took some yeast and added sugar, eggs, flour, raisins, and candied fruit. The improvised dessert was whisker-licking good! The chef who invented it was named Antonio. His dessert became known as "Toni's bread," or *"pan de Toni/ panettone"* in Italian.

THE HALL OF CARYATIDS

The caryatids that give this room its name are sculpted figures that have served as columns in this part of the Royal Palace since the 1700s. During World War II, the palace was bombed, and the room was largely destroyed. While the room was restored, the ceiling and floor were not decorated as grandly as the originals, in testimony to the tragedy of war.

WHO WANTS TO FRAME GERONIMO?

Poor Scooter wiped the tears from his snout. "Some rat stole the secret recipe! That scroll was priceless to me and to the city of Milan! It was the only unique, original, inimitable, super-old, extremely precious scroll that the recipe for panettone had been written on for the very first time!"

Thea hugged him. "Don't worry, Scooter,

Be strong! Sob! Oh, Scooter! Don't worry!

we're here for you! We've solved cases as **hard** as aged Parmesan. We'll help you!"

"Rodent's honor!" I added with a nod. "Operation: Secret Recipe starts now."

Hercule gave Scooter a pat on the back. "Thea's right, we're *great* at solving **mysteries**. Could we get a look at the videos from those security cameras? They might help us catch the *sneaky little rat* who stole the recipe — red-pawed."

We'll help you!

We're great at solving mysteries!

As we watched the security **VIDEOS**, our jaws dropped like string cheese melting in the sun . . . **especially mine!**

Watching the videos left me completely *squeakless*!

The thief was my size, with the same color fur. Under his janitorial disguise, he wore a green suit like mine—with the same red tie! And he wore a pair of ROUND glasses on his snout, too.

Sound familiar?

Basically, the thief looked exactly like ME!

Even though I could hardly believe my eyes, I also couldn't help noticing that the thief was much more agile than me—he'd leaped right over the security Gate!

Who wants to frame me?

Hercule twisted his tail into a knot. "I can't believe it! Someone wants to FRAME Geronimo Stilton! Who? How? And above all . . . WHY?"

Benjamin and Bugsy both tugged

at my sleeve. "Uncle Geronimo, DID YOU SEE? Before leaving the room, the thief threw something in the GARBAGE!"

I shook my snout. *"What do you mean?"*

They dragged me over to the screen, and rewound to a split second that none of us had noticed: after the heist, the thief threw his blue uniform in the garbage!

Hercule clapped his paws. "Well done, mouselets! That was some fabumouse investigative work!"

He scampered over to paw through the garbage.

"For all the fondue in New Mouse City, here's that rotten rat's uniform!" Hercule squeaked. He pulled the uniform out of the trash and immediately noticed that there was a folded piece of paper in one of the pockets. "Ah, that miserable mouse was

DISTRACTED and forgot something," he said, calling the rest of us over to look.

We all gathered around the paper . . .

What is this paper?

It was a map of Milan, and someone had marked it with big red **X s**. Next to each *X* were mysterious numbers: **10:00**;

10:10; 10:20; 10:30 . . .

I tugged at my whiskers. What could it mean?

HMMM . . .

It's a map of Milan!

HMM . . .

HMM . . .

HMM . . .

HMM . . .

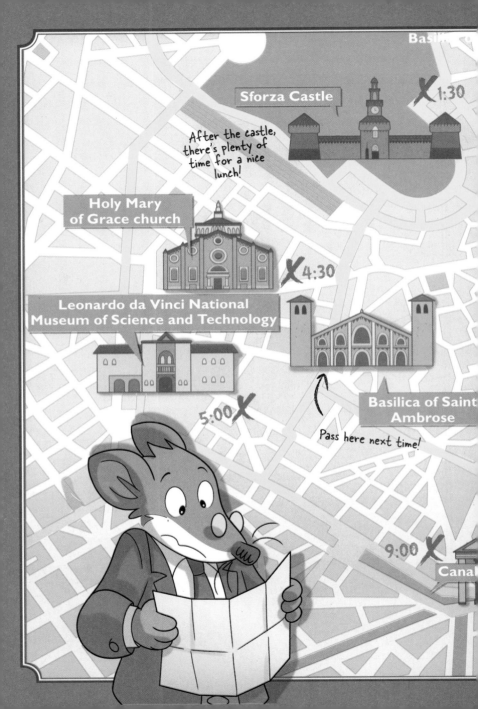

MAP OF MILAN
Brera Art Gallery
10:30
La Scala Theater
Milan Cathedral (Duomo)
King Vittorio Emanuele Gallery
10:20
10:00
Climb the cathedral for a nice photo!
Royal Palace
10:10
Prime objective: Royal Palace!

THE HUNT FOR THE THIEF

I pointed to the red numbers written on the map. "Crusty cat litter, these mysterious **numbers** are actually times! Maybe the thief has appointments all over Milan . . . but with who?"

"Geronimo, you big lump of SMARTY SWISS!" Hercule exclaimed. "Come on, let's catch this thief! The next appointment on the map is nearby, at the King Vittorio Emanuele Gallery at ten twenty."

Bruce Hyena leaped to his paws. "It's in less than five minutes—let's hurry! The secret recipe waits for no mouse!"

I was about to **SCAMPER** outside, but Thea grabbed my tail.

"Hold it right there, big brother! Where do you think you're going? If someone is trying to frame you, we can't let you be recognized! You need a disguise." She put her jacket on me.

"Cheese and crackers, it's a bit tight— but it's better than nothing."

Uncle Grayfur plopped his SAILOR'S CAP on my head, and Aunt Sweetfur wrapped my snout in her PURPLE shawl. Benjamin lent me a pair of his pants, which fit me almost like **shorts**. And for the finishing touch, Petunia Pretty Paws set her pink *sunglasses* on my snout!

Think anyone will recognize me?

Now no one would recognize me . . . but I looked like a **crazy cheesebrain**!

There was no time to worry about that as we scurried out of the Royal Palace.

Scooter hollered, "Follow me—we can still make it!"

He headed toward a giant archway that led to the other side of the square. There was the Gallery: a big, beautiful shopping center!

We came to a stop right in the middle of the Gallery.

Just then, I spotted a mouse that looked just like me, surrounded by a **CROWD** of admirers. He was signing **aut°GRaPHS**!

He squeaked proudly, "Yes, I wrote all of those *books*—because I am the famous Geronimo Stilton!"

I twisted my tail into a knot, watching the

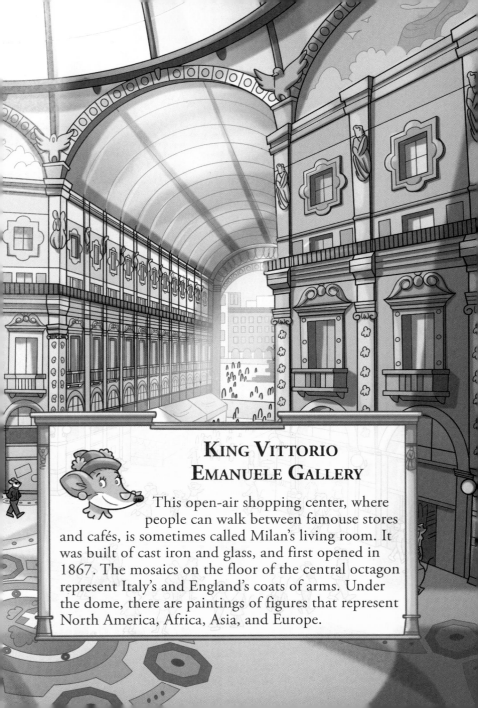

KING VITTORIO EMANUELE GALLERY

This open-air shopping center, where people can walk between famouse stores and cafés, is sometimes called Milan's living room. It was built of cast iron and glass, and first opened in 1867. The mosaics on the floor of the central octagon represent Italy's and England's coats of arms. Under the dome, there are paintings of figures that represent North America, Africa, Asia, and Europe.

imposter brag and kiss onlookers' paws. What a rat! There's nothing that bothers me more than dishonesty. It really **toasts my cheese**!

Suddenly, a mouse cried, "Holey cheese, Geronimo Stilton is a **thief**! As he kissed my **Paw,** he stole my ruby ring!"

The thief gave a satisfied laugh.

An autograph?

Me, too!

What a pleasure!

Wow, Geronimo Stilton!

Ha ha ha!

Then he darted away as fast as his paws would take him, zigzagging through the crowd. **A L L** of the rodents nearby tried to grab him, but he was too speedy! He zoomed off, calling, "Na-na-na-na-meow-meow—I mean, *na-na-na-na-foo-foo!*"

I threw my paws into the air.

For the love of cheese, we had missed the **thief** by a whisker!

Na-na-na-na-meow-meow!

I Am a
Serious Mouse!

Without wasting a moment, Hercule pulled out the map. The thief's next APPOINTMENT was at La Scala Theater at 10:30.

Thea LOOKED me up and down, shaking her snout. "Before we go, you need a better disguise! We'll have to buy something . . ."

Rodent friends, you may already know that my uncle Samuel S. Stingysnout is a tremendmouse **cheapskate**. Believe it or not, his son Stevie is even worse!

Stevie held up his paws in alarm. "Buy something? You mean, spending and squandering?" he squeaked. "OHHHHH,

I can hardly believe my ears! Not for all the mozzarella in Milan!"

He grabbed the previous day's newspaper from the garbage, poked two **holes** in it, and draped it over my snout. Then he brushed his paws together, **SATISFIED**. "There you go! All you need to disguise Geronimo is a nice old NEWSPAPER. The less you see of him, the better—and it's FREE!"

We all rolled our eyes.

"**NO**, Stevie, that's not going to work," Thea said with a sigh.

This newspaper is perfect!

What's your plan?

There, done!

Argh!

I was starting to feel desperate!

"Please, I just want to look dignified," I begged, pulling the newspaper off my snout. "After all, I do run the most famouse newspaper in **NEW MOUSE CITY**! I'm an intellectual mouse—I have a reputation to protect."

Hercule squeezed my shoulder. "**Geronimo**, leave it to me!"

I squeaked a sigh of relief. After all, Hercule is a private investigator. He's known for his disguises! He pawed through the pockets of his yellow trench coat and finally pulled SOMETHING out.

"Look here, Stilton. You'll never believe it—I have the perfect costume!"

I was HAPPIER than a mouse in a fondue factory. "What is it?"

Hercule winked at me and began to

INFLATE the costume with a little bike pump.

Crusty cat litter, this didn't look good!

A moment later, everything became clear. It was an ENORMOUSE inflatable panettone, complete with fake candied fruit, fake raisins, fake sickening vanilla scent, and a **ridiculous** fake lace doily that looked like a skirt!

Hercule grinned proudly. "It's a *PANETTONE* costume! Do you like it, Stilton? It fits perfectly with Milan and this mysterious case. Plus, dressed up like this, pawsitively no one will recognize you!"

I waved my paws and shook my snout. "I want a serious *costume*! I am a serious mouse! Why is this so hard for everyone to understand? **I can't wear that!**"

Benjamin squeaked up. "Umm, Uncle Geronimo? If I were you, I would put on the panettone costume right away. We're late!"

I sighed. As usual, Benjamin was right . . .

So I swallowed my mousely pride, put on the panettone costume, and headed toward La Scala Theater. THUNDERING CATTAILS, I felt ridiculous!

When we arrived in the square, Squeaky and Squeakette cried in unison, "There's the famouse Classical Dance Academy! Oh, we would love to go there!"

If I catch you . . .

Don't be like that, Stilton!

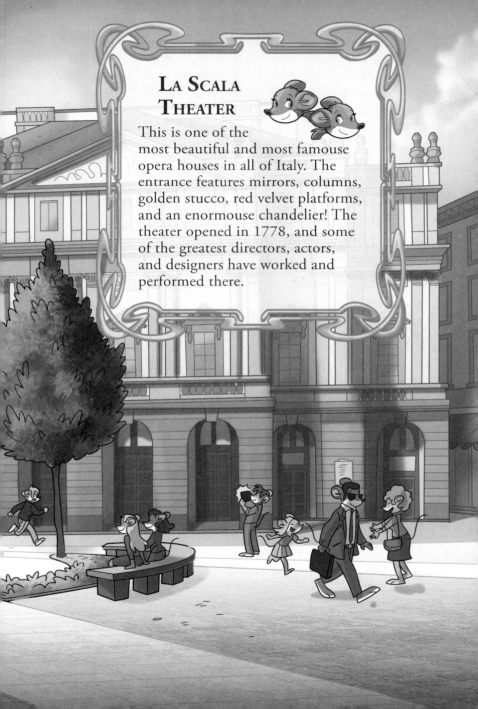

LA SCALA THEATER

This is one of the most beautiful and most famous opera houses in all of Italy. The entrance features mirrors, columns, golden stucco, red velvet platforms, and an enormouse chandelier! The theater opened in 1778, and some of the greatest directors, actors, and designers have worked and performed there.

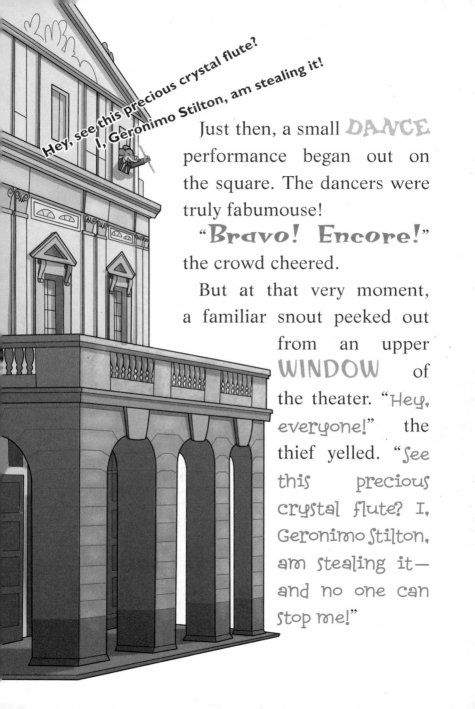

Hey, see this precious crystal flute? I, Geronimo Stilton, am stealing it!

Just then, a small DANCE performance began out on the square. The dancers were truly fabumouse!

"Bravo! Encore!" the crowd cheered.

But at that very moment, a familiar snout peeked out from an upper WINDOW of the theater. "Hey, everyone!" the thief yelled. "See this precious crystal flute? I, Geronimo Stilton, am stealing it—and no one can stop me!"

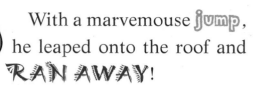

With a marvemouse **jump**, he leaped onto the roof and **RAN AWAY**!

The rodents in the crowd shook their snouts in dismay.

"Geronimo Stilton really is a **thief**! Putrid Parmesan, what a disgrace!"

I felt my fur turn **red** with embarrassment. For the first time, I was happy to be dressed up like **panettone**!

Even so, I couldn't help thinking that something was awfully odd about that thief. He seemed almost **too** agile . . . **Strange!**

Bravo!

Look!

The thief!

It's Stilton!

A Dented Can of Tuna

Scooter jumped on his red moped and darted off, yelling, "The next appointment on the map is ten fifty at the Brera Art Gallery! Follow me, friends!"

A few moments later, Scooter parked in front of a large old building. When we caught up, he **explained**, "This is the Brera Art Gallery,

Quick!

where you can admire **PaiNtiNGS** that are famouse all around the world."

Together, we walked through the gallery rooms. **Cheese niblets**, there were so many fabumouse works of art here!

But no matter how hard we looked, there was no trace of the THIEF. The only thing we found was a dented can of **TUNA FISH** in one corner. Could the thief have dropped it?

STRANGE!

Scooter thought quietly, twirling his whiskers. "I'll bet the thief has already left."

"Hmmm," I said. "But the appointment on the map says ten fifty, right? He should be here **now**!"

We're here!

The art gallery!

Come on!

Hurry up!

THE BRERA ART GALLERY

The art gallery is on the first floor of the Brera Palace. Beyond the statue of Napoleon in the beautiful courtyard, there are two stairways that lead up to the gallery. In these rooms are the works of some of the greatest Italian artists, including Mantegna, Raphael, and Piero della Francesca.

It smells like vanilla!

I borrowed a magnifying glass from *Hercule,* since he always keeps one in his pocket. I used it to peer more closely at the **map** of Milan. Cheese and crackers! I finally understood!

There was a **coffee stain** right above the time of the Art Gallery appointment. That's why the writing was blurred—I had read it wrong!

The Brera appointment was at 10:40, not 10:50!

"Gobs of Gouda, we got here *late!*" I squeaked frantically. "We need to get our tails to the next appointment. It's at SFORZA CASTLE at one thirty!"

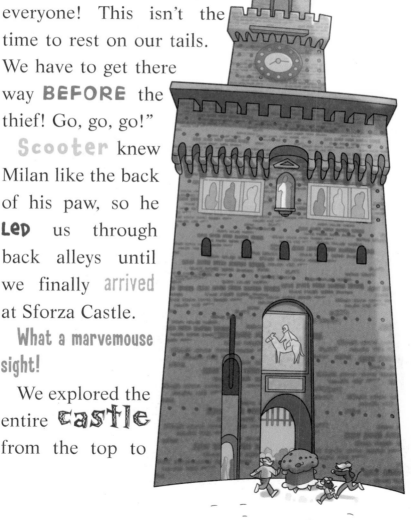

Bruce Hyena took charge immediately. "Shake a paw, everyone! This isn't the time to rest on our tails. We have to get there way **BEFORE** the thief! Go, go, go!"

Scooter knew Milan like the back of his paw, so he **LED** us through back alleys until we finally arrived at Sforza Castle.

What a marvemouse sight!

We explored the entire **castle** from the top to

the bottom. We even staked out places to wait for the thief as 1:30 drew closer, but we didn't spot him anywhere.

I was starting to feel like the cheese was **slipping off** of my cracker!

At last, Hercule suggested, "Let's check the castle's Egyptian Museum. There are tons of fabumouse treasures in there—maybe there's something the thief would try to steal."

Here's the fake Geronimo!

SFORZA CASTLE

Built by the Visconti, the rulers of
Milan in the 1300s, the castle was later
enlarged by the Sforza family. The Sforzas
wanted the castle to be both beautiful and useful
in defending Milan. The castle was later occupied
by the Spanish, Austrian, and French soldiers who
dominated the city. Around one hundred years ago,
it was restored by a man named Luca Beltrami;
today, the castle is home to libraries and museums
that are open to everyone.

Here is the real
Geronimo—me!

Trap added, "Ooh, and I'll bet there are MUMMIES! Doesn't that sound mousetastic, Cousin?"

That didn't sound mousetastic at all!

Dear reader, you may not know this . . . but I am PETRIFIED of mummies!

As soon as we entered the mouseum, we heard the guards squeaking in alarm.

"That rat stole the statue of the goddess Bastet!"

"He always seemed like such a respectable RODENT . . ."

Waaaah!

Umm . . .

He stole the statue!

Argh!

Strange!

"But he's a thief!"

"What did he say his name was?"

"Stilton, Geronimo Stilton!"

"Ooh, if I get my paws on him . . ."

Holey cheese! I tucked my tail farther into the **PANETTONE** costume—I couldn't risk being recognized!

I also couldn't help noticing the thief's mysterious target. Why would he steal the statue of the goddess Bastet? She's a cat-goddess!

THE STATUE OF THE GODDESS BASTET

Bastet was a popular goddess of Ancient Egypt who took the form of a cat. The daughter of Ra, the sun god, she was considered to be the goddess of the home (among other things), protecting houses from evil spirits and disease.

The Ancient Egyptians adored cats, which defended their homes and crops from thieving vermin. They dedicated temples, poems, and statues to various cats, and even buried them in special cemeteries and embalmed them like the pharaohs!

A GORGONZOLA ICE CREAM CONE

We hightailed it out of the musuem and tried to **follow** the thief's trail, but he had vanished! Instead, we headed to the next appointment on the map: **Holy Mary of Grace church** at 4:30. (I was excited, because that's where Leonardo da Vinci's famouse mural, *The Last Supper*, is located!)

But it was hard to get too excited, because my morale was at rock bottom. That thieving rat was ruining my REPUTATION!

Plus, I was hungrier than a cat in a cage. We'd skipped lunch to chase after the thief!

Just then Aunt Sweetfur offered me an enormouse Gorgonzola ice cream cone, with an edible **umbrella**, caramel *sauce*, whipped cream, a cookie, almonds, and a **CHERRY** on top.

"Dear Nephew, eat some **ice cream**—it will fill you up and give you energy!" she squeaked kindly.

I threw my paws around her. "Thank you. I really needed this!"

As my friends and family entered the large room where The Last Supper mural was located, I stayed outside and chowed down. (You're not allowed inside a mouseum with an ice cream cone. Every respectable rodent knows that!)

I ate QUICKLY so that I could see the famouse painting—I adore Leonardo da Vinci!

Suddenly, I felt someone tap me on the back. "Is that you, Stilton?"

I spun on my paws, STUTTERING

THE LAST SUPPER

This is a large painted mural in the refectory of the Holy Mary of Grace church in Milan. Leonardo da Vinci used an oil painting technique that was different from the typical fresco, so this masterpiece has lost some of its detail and coloring over time. But today, after many restorations, it remains an amazing sight!

How marvemouse!

It's so beautiful!

in surprise, "Y-yes, I'm Stilton, Geronimo Stilt—"

But I never finished my sentence, because before my eyes I saw . . . me! Crusty cheese crumpets!

Of course, it wasn't actually me. It was the thief!

He snatched the ICE CREAM CONE from my paw, snickering. "Thanks, cheesebrain!"

Then he scampered away, laughing at me and leaving drops of ice cream trailing behind him. Rats—I wasn't done eating that!

As he fled, a fish bone tumbled out of his pocket.

Strange!

Ha, ha, ha!

DROPS OF ICE CREAM!

Once my friends and family came back outside, we followed the drops of GORGONZOLA ice cream until we arrived at a large door. It was the entrance to the

> ## LEONARDO DA VINCI NATIONAL MUSEUM OF SCIENCE
> ### AND
> ## TECHNOLOGY

We entered on TIPTOE, quiet as mice . . .

I couldn't believe it — we had finally caught the thief **red-pawed** as he stopped to finish **my** ice cream (inside a museum, no less)!

For the love of all things cheesy, it was really him!

Trap's eyes were wide. "If you weren't here next to me, Gerry Berry, I would think that *he* was really **YOU**—I mean, that you are **him**—I mean—"

Thea cut him off. "Yes, we get it. But now let's get **him**!"

Thea jumped out

LEONARDO DA VINCI NATIONAL MUSEUM OF SCIENCE AND TECHNOLOGY

In the rooms of an ancient Milanese monastery, there is a museum dedicated to science and technology. It is named after Leonardo da Vinci, who was not only a painter, but a scholar of nature and inventive technology. The museum contains 130 models inspired by the drawings of his machines, like the famouse "helicopter" (the Aerial Screw).

and ran toward the thief. "**PAWS UP!**"

Stunned, he cried, "Meowww—I mean, squeak!"

STRANGE!

He turned and tried to run, but slipped on a **GLOB** of Gorgonzola ice cream and fell snout over paws into a model of one of da Vinci's machines. Before he could squeak, his tail got caught between the **gears**!

Grandfather William stood snout-to-snout

The thief slipped on a glob of ice cream.... then he....➤

Help!

fell snout over paws into one of da Vinci's models!

Eeeek!

with the thief. "Now *confess*—no more lies! Tell us who you are, and why you're trying to pass as my grandson!"

The `thief` paused for a moment, as if he were *SIZING* up the situation and deciding what tactic to use. I couldn't help shaking in my fur. Who knew what this **rascally rat** was going to do next?

Sly guy!!

Confess!

Umm . . .

Who are you?

Get squeaking!

There's no way out!

Finally, his tail got caught between the gears!

WHICH ONE OF YOU IS GERONIMO STILTON?

Before I knew it, the thief had grabbed my arm and pulled me out of my panettone costume! Then he yanked my tail and sent me into a spin, until he and I were whirling around together like a top. Cheese and crackers, I'd never been so dizzy in my life!

Whirrrr!
Whirrrrrrrr!
Whirrrrr!

While we spun around and around and around, he SANG softly. (His voice sounded just like mine, too—he was even

tone deaf, like me! Squeak!)

> "Do–do–do–do–dooooo,
> Now what will you do?
> They can't tell who is who!
> Geronimo Stilton, which one are you?"

When we finally stopped spinning, we stood **Snout-to-Snout**, staring each other in the eyes. I was furious—and a little queasy!

Just then, I noticed a strange, fishy smell . . .

Who are you?

Who are you?!

I knew that **I** was **ME** and that **HE** was **HIM**, but my friends and family were more mixed-up than a mozzarella milkshake. They all started squeaking at once. "Which one of you is the real Geronimo Stilton?"

Anxious, I shouted, "I am! I'm the real Geronimo Stilton! Not him!"

But the thief also started to shout. "Dear friends, don't believe this imposter—I am the real Geronimo Stilton!" Then he turned and pulled my whisker. "How **Dare** you pretend to be me!"

Everyone began to **circle** around us, muttering, "Umm, that one there is **SHORTER** than Geronimo . . . or maybe he's **taller**? No, no, no, you can tell that the real Geronimo is that one with the longer **whiskers**. Or is he the one whose ears stick out more? It's impossible to tell them apart—moldy mozzarella, this is hard!"

I continued to repeat desperately, "Friends, how can you not recognize me? I am the real Geronimo, me! Squeeeak!"

The thief smiled under his whiskers and clapped a paw against my back. "Hey, rat, it seems like no one can tell which of us is the real Geronimo. What we need is a competition—an official squeakdown! HA, HA, HA!"

The thief began to ask questions as fast as he could squeak. "What is your

Which is the real one?

Holey cheese, he's the real one!

No, it's the other one!

grandfather's exact date of birth? What is the exact zip code where your cousin Stevie lives? Exactly how old was your niece Squeakette when she had her tonsils taken out?"

That wasn't all. Cheese niblets, this rat went on and on and on! "Exactly how many steps are on the staircase of Geronimo Stilton's house? Exactly how many days ago did he last go to the dentist? Exactly how much did his last electric bill cost?"

Cheese and crackers, I felt like I was drowning in questions! "Umm, I don't

remember exactly . . . but I would say . . . well, who knows . . . uh, the answer is on the tip of my tongue . . . squeak, who can remember all those details?"

That rat, on the other paw, knew ALL the details of my private life!

For the love of cheese, he must have **studied**!

With a smug look on his snout, he boasted, "I have just proven that I am Geronimo Stilton — and he isn't! The facts don't lie!"

I watched in shock as my family and friends **nodded** slowly. "We have to admit, you know **everything** about Geronimo's private life. This other

But I . . .

You know nothing!

rodent was more **confused** than a mouse in a maze . . ."

The only one who didn't squeak up was my nephew **Benjamin**. He looked back and forth between me and the thief, muttering, "**HMMM** . . ."

I put my paws together and begged, "PLEASE, BENJAMIN, YOU BELIEVE ME, RIGHT?"

But the imposter, imitating my voice perfectly, chimed in. "Benjamin, don't listen to a word he squeaks! I'm your real uncle — Stilton, Geronimo Stilton!"

A FELINE FRIGHT!

The fake Geronimo TRIED to hug Benjamin, but my nephew took a step back and said, "If you're really my uncle, tell me how many buttons you accidentally ripped off your jacket this morning before you left."

The thief frowned. "Umm, right . . . the jacket! Of course . . . certainly . . . this morning I ripped two buttons off my jacket . . . just as I was leaving. What a cheesebrain!"

Benjamin's eyes lit up and he squeaked, "Wrong! You are not my uncle! You are not the real Geronimo! The REAL Geronimo didn't rip any buttons off his **jacket** this morning! He ripped three buttons off his *pajamas*!"

Hercule clapped his paws and cheered. "Benjamin, that was FABUMOUSE!

I would like to hire you as my **assistant**!"

Without a moment to spare, Hercule and all my friends jumped on top of the fake Geronimo to keep him from escaping. He leaped nimbly away yelling,

"Na-na-na-na-meow-meow!"

Na-na-na-na-meow-meow!

I'm going to get you!

Stop him!

You rat!

My fur stood on end. "**WHAT?** Did you say, 'Na-na-na-na-meow-meow'?"

What a feline fright! That rat . . . was actually a cat!

Thundering cattails, that's why he was so **LIGHT ON HIS PAWS**! That's why he had been carrying that **can** of tuna! That's why he stole the cat-goddess Bastet statue! That's why he dropped a **FISH BONE**! And that's why his whiskers smelled like fish!

He gave us a sly smile. "Okay, fine, you rats have figured me out! I'm a **PIRATE CAT**! Na-na-na-na-meow-meow! We had a perfect plan—and you rodents **ruined** it!"

The cat continued:

"**1.)** We wanted to send Geronimo Stilton to JAIL. That's why we tried to frame you, rat!

2.) Without you, *The Rodent's Gazette* would *fail*!

3.) Without *The Rodent's Gazette*, no one would keep the rodents of Mouse Island INFORMED!

4.) With you mice in the dark, us pirate cats could get to the shores of Mouse Island undetected!

5.) We could steal the rodents' treasures and, best of all, we would have all the tasty rodents we could eat! Yum!"

Give up!

My whiskers where trembling with rage. Who did this crazy cat think he was?

I stepped forward, gathered my courage, and squeaked, "Give up, cat! It's over! Give us back the secret PANETTONE recipe and all the other treasures you stole!"

But instead, the cat pulled off his mouse

costume and **RaN away!** Luckily, the ruby **RING** he'd stolen from the mouse at the mall, the precious **FLUTE** he'd taken from La Scala Theater, the Bastet statue, and the ancient **SCROLL** with the panettone recipe all tumbled out of his disguise.

I gathered up the stolen objects so I could give them all back to their rightful owners. Finally, I pawed the scroll to Scooter. "Holey cheese — operation: Secret Recipe is complete!"

A HISTORIC BUILDING

Scooter **invited** all of us—plus our new Milanese friends—to his mousehole for dinner that night. "Let's celebrate with a Milanese meal: **rice** with saffron, OSSO BUCO, and of course, Panettone with mascarpone cream!"

Trap licked his whiskers. "*YUM, YUM, YUM!*"

Once everyone had arrived, Scooter held up the **ancient** panettone recipe and gave a little speech.

"Dear friends, I can't thank you enough for tracking down the secret panettone recipe, not to mention all of the other stolen objects!" Scooter squeaked with a cheesy smile. "Tomorrow at the Royal Palace, I can finally present this precious DOCUMENT to the press.

It's going to be a truly marvemouse day!"

We all cheered and clapped our paws.

Trap squinted, trying to read the recipe. "What language is this written in? I can't understand a cheese rind of what it says!"

I peered closely at the unrolled scroll. Cheesy cream puffs, my crazy cousin was **RIGHT**! Had we gone on a wild mouse chase just to track down something unreadable? *Squeak!*

Scooter held up his paws. "Don't worry, friends! The recipe is written in *Meneghino*, an ancient language of Milan. The time has finally come to translate it, and luckily, my **friends** from the Meneghina Family Society* can help. They're experts on Milanese history."

*The Meneghina Family Society is an association that promotes awareness about Milanese culture.

Moldy mozzarella, what a relief! For a second there, I'd thought I was going to toss my cheese.

Two rodents stepped forward and began to leaf through a stack of **books** and dictionaries on Scooter's table. Before I could gobble down my fourth slice of panettone (it really was TASTY!) they had translated the precious document. I was so excited I could hardly squeak! Of course, the recipe itself was nothing new, but what a MOUSETASTIC cultural artifact!

Huh?

We'll translate it!

HERE'S THE TRANSLATION OF THE FAMOUSE PANETTONE RECIPE!

Not too hard or too soft, not too creamy or too dry, not too sweet or too greasy, this is the perfect dessert. Mice from miles around all agree! Majestic but simple, topped with candied fruit, this is tasty and refined, fabumousely filling, and forever a favorite. This cake should always be made with fresh, quality ingredients: sugar, eggs, butter, flour, candied fruit, and plenty of raisins. This is definitely a dessert to squeak about!

Yum!

GOOD-BYE, MILAN!

When it was time to **return** home, all our new Milanese friends were sad to see us go. Scooter **hugged** me. "Geronimo, please come back anytime you want—you're always WELCOME in Milan!"

I smiled. "My friend, we will definitely see each other again! Please come visit us in New Mouse City. And since I never actually

got to **see** *The Last Supper*, I'll definitely come back to Milan soon!"

Scooter laughed.

"It was **fabumouse** to meet you," I went on. "After all, we have the same interest in books and the same passion for history. It's not every day you meet a mouse with such *good taste*!"

Scooter **darted** off on his red moped, waving a paw and calling, "Good-bye!"

As we climbed back into the camper, I

Come back anytime you want!

Good-bye!

couldn't help thinking about our fabumouse adventure. I had made so many new **friends** in Milan, and discovered so many new things . . .

. . . like how *whisker-licking good* panettone is! **YUM!**

Plus, Operation: Secret Recipe was a success! And along the way, I'd gotten to see famouse sights like La Scala Theater and Sforza Castle. I'd never forget climbing to the top of the Duomo di Milano and admiring the view. **What a city!** I hadn't wanted to come on this trip in the first place, but now I was so glad I'd let my family and friends **twist my paw.**

milan is a truly mousetastic place!

Dear readers, if you ever have the chance to visit Milan, get your tail in gear and go! I'll bet you'd have a wonderful adventure there, just like we did . . .

RODENT'S HONOR!

Yum!

Be sure to read all my fabumouse adventures!

#1 Lost Treasure of the Emerald Eye

#2 The Curse of the Cheese Pyramid

#3 Cat and Mouse in a Haunted House

#4 I'm Too Fond of My Fur!

#5 Four Mice Deep in the Jungle

#6 Paws Off, Cheddarface!

#7 Red Pizzas for a Blue Count

#8 Attack of the Bandit Cats

#9 A Fabumouse Vacation for Geronimo

#10 All Because of a Cup of Coffee

#11 It's Halloween, You 'Fraidy Mouse!

#12 Merry Christmas, Geronimo!

#13 The Phantom of the Subway

#14 The Temple of the Ruby of Fire

#15 The Mona Mousa Code

#16 A Cheese-Colored Camper

#17 Watch Your Whiskers, Stilton!

#18 Shipwreck on the Pirate Islands

#19 My Name Is Stilton, Geronimo Stilton

#20 Surf's Up, Geronimo!

#21 The Wild, Wild West

#22 The Secret of Cacklefur Castle

A Christmas Tale

#23 Valentine's Day Disaster

#24 Field Trip to Niagara Falls

#25 The Search for Sunken Treasure

#26 The Mummy with No Name

#27 The Christmas Toy Factory

#28 Wedding Crasher

#29 Down and Out Down Under

#30 The Mouse Island Marathon

#31 The Mysterious Cheese Thief

Christmas Catastrophe

#32 Valley of the Giant Skeletons

#33 Geronimo and the Gold Medal Mystery

#34 Geronimo Stilton, Secret Agent

#35 A Very Merry Christmas

#36 Geronimo's Valentine

#37 The Race Across America

#38 A Fabumouse School Adventure

#39 Singing Sensation

#40 The Karate Mouse

#41 Mighty Mount Kilimanjaro

#42 The Peculiar Pumpkin Thief

#43 I'm Not a Supermouse!

#44 The Giant Diamond Robbery

#45 Save the White Whale!

#46 The Haunted Castle

#47 Run for the Hills, Geronimo!

#48 The Mystery in Venice

#49 The Way of the Samurai

#50 This Hotel Is Haunted!

#51 The Enormouse Pearl Heist

#52 Mouse in Space!

#53 Rumble in the Jungle

#54 Get into Gear, Stilton!

#55 The Golden Statue Plot

#56 Flight of the Red Bandit

Special Edition!

The Hunt for the Golden Book

#57 The Stinky Cheese Vacation

#58 The Super Chef Contest

#59 Welcome to Moldy Manor

Special Edition!

The Hunt for the Curious Cheese

#60 The Treasure of Easter Island

#61 Mouse House Hunter

#62 Mouse Overboard!

Special Edition!

The Hunt for the Secret Papyrus

#63 The Cheese Experiment

#64 Magical Mission

#65 Bollywood Burglary

Special Edition!

The Hunt for the Hundredth Key

#66 Operation: Secret Recipe

Up Next!

#67 The Chocolate Chase

MEET
Geronimo Stiltonord

He is a mouseking — the Geronimo Stilton of the ancient far north! He lives with his brawny and brave clan in the village of Mouseborg. From sailing frozen waters to facing fiery dragons, every day is an adventure for the micekings!

#1 Attack of the Dragons

#2 The Famouse Fjord Race

#3 Pull the Dragon's Tooth!

#4 Stay Strong, Geronimo!

#5 The Mysterious Message

#6 The Helmet Holdup

Don't miss any of these exciting Thea Sisters adventures!

Thea Stilton and the Dragon's Code

Thea Stilton and the Mountain of Fire

Thea Stilton and the Ghost of the Shipwreck

Thea Stilton and the Secret City

Thea Stilton and the Mystery in Paris

Thea Stilton and the Cherry Blossom Adventure

Thea Stilton and the Star Castaways

Thea Stilton: Big Trouble in the Big Apple

Thea Stilton and the Ice Treasure

Thea Stilton and the Secret of the Old Castle

Thea Stilton and the Blue Scarab Hunt

Thea Stilton and the Prince's Emerald

Thea Stilton and the Mystery on the Orient Express

Thea Stilton and the Dancing Shadows

Thea Stilton and the Legend of the Fire Flowers

Thea Stilton and the Spanish Dance Mission

Thea Stilton and the Journey to the Lion's Den

Thea Stilton and the
Great Tulip Heist

Thea Stilton and the
Chocolate Sabotage

Thea Stilton and the
Missing Myth

Thea Stilton and the
Lost Letters

Thea Stilton and the
Tropical Treasure

Thea Stilton and the
Hollywood Hoax

Thea Stilton and the
Madagascar Madness

Thea Stilton and the
Frozen Fiasco

Thea Stilton and the
Venice Masquerade

And check out my fabumouse special editions!

THEA STILTON:
THE JOURNEY
TO ATLANTIS

THEA STILTON:
THE SECRET OF
THE FAIRIES

THEA STILTON:
THE SECRET OF
THE SNOW

THEA STILTON:
THE CLOUD
CASTLE

THEA STILTON:
THE TREASURE
OF THE SEA

THEA STILTON:
THE LAND OF
FLOWERS

Don't miss any of my special edition adventures!

THE KINGDOM OF FANTASY

THE QUEST FOR PARADISE:
THE RETURN TO THE KINGDOM OF FANTASY

THE AMAZING VOYAGE:
THE THIRD ADVENTURE IN THE KINGDOM OF FANTASY

THE DRAGON PROPHECY:
THE FOURTH ADVENTURE IN THE KINGDOM OF FANTASY

THE VOLCANO OF FIRE:
THE FIFTH ADVENTURE IN THE KINGDOM OF FANTASY

THE SEARCH FOR TREASURE:
THE SIXTH ADVENTURE IN THE KINGDOM OF FANTASY

THE ENCHANTED CHARMS:
THE SEVENTH ADVENTURE IN THE KINGDOM OF FANTASY

THE PHOENIX OF DESTINY:
AN EPIC KINGDOM OF FANTASY ADVENTURE

THE HOUR OF MAGIC:
THE EIGHTH ADVENTURE IN THE KINGDOM OF FANTASY

THE WIZARD'S WAND:
THE NINTH ADVENTURE IN THE KINGDOM OF FANTASY

THE SHIP OF SECRETS:
THE TENTH ADVENTURE IN THE KINGDOM OF FANTASY

THE DRAGON OF FORTUNE:
AN EPIC KINGDOM OF FANTASY ADVENTURE

THE JOURNEY THROUGH TIME

BACK IN TIME:
THE SECOND JOURNEY THROUGH TIME

THE RACE AGAINST TIME:
THE THIRD JOURNEY THROUGH TIME

LOST IN TIME:
THE FOURTH JOURNEY THROUGH TIME

MEET GERONIMO STILTONIX

He is a spacemouse — the Geronimo Stilton of a parallel universe! He is captain of the spaceship *MouseStar 1*. While flying through the cosmos, he visits distant planets and meets crazy aliens. His adventures are out of this world!

#1 Alien Escape

#2 You're Mine, Captain!

#3 Ice Planet Adventure

#4 The Galactic Goal

#5 Rescue Rebellion

#6 The Underwater Planet

#7 Beware! Space Junk!

#8 Away in a Star Sled

#9 Slurp Monster Showdown

#10 Pirate Spacecat Attack

#11 We'll Bite Your Tail, Geronimo!

ABOUT THE AUTHOR

Born in New Mouse City, Mouse Island, **GERONIMO STILTON** is Rattus Emeritus of Mousomorphic Literature and of Neo-Ratonic Comparative Philosophy. For the past twenty years, he has been running *The Rodent's Gazette*, New Mouse City's most widely read daily newspaper.

Stilton was awarded the Ratitzer Prize for his scoops on *The Curse of the Cheese Pyramid* and *The Search for Sunken Treasure*. He has also received the Andersen 2000 Prize for Personality of the Year. One of his bestsellers won the 2002 eBook Award for world's best ratlings' electronic book. His works have been published all over the globe.

In his spare time, Mr. Stilton collects antique cheese rinds and plays golf. But what he most enjoys is telling stories to his nephew Benjamin.

1. Main entrance
2. Printing presses (where the books and newspaper are printed)
3. Accounts department
4. Editorial room (where the editors, illustrators, and designers work)
5. Geronimo Stilton's office
6. Helicopter landing pad

THE RODENT'S GAZETTE

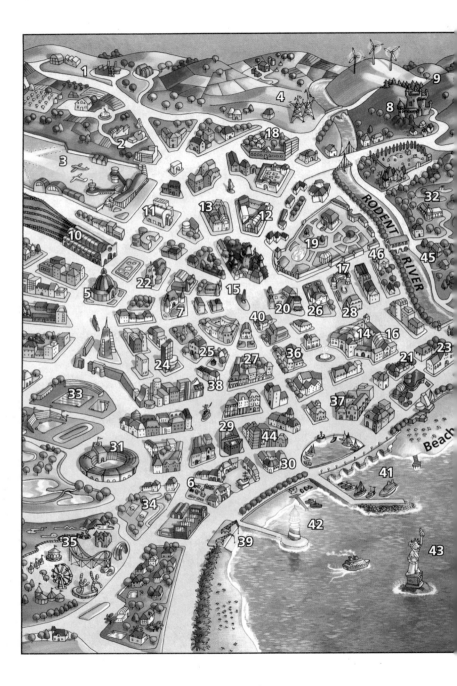

Map of New Mouse City

Map of Mouse Island

1. Big Ice Lake
2. Frozen Fur Peak
3. Slipperyslopes Glacier
4. Coldcreeps Peak
5. Ratzikistan
6. Transratania
7. Mount Vamp
8. Roastedrat Volcano
9. Brimstone Lake
10. Poopedcat Pass
11. Stinko Peak
12. Dark Forest
13. Vain Vampires Valley
14. Goose Bumps Gorge
15. The Shadow Line Pass
16. Penny Pincher Castle
17. Nature Reserve Park
18. Las Ratayas Marinas
19. Fossil Forest
20. Lake Lake
21. Lake Lakelake
22. Lake Lakelakelake
23. Cheddar Crag
24. Cannycat Castle
25. Valley of the Giant Sequoia
26. Cheddar Springs
27. Sulfurous Swamp
28. Old Reliable Geyser
29. Vole Vale
30. Ravingrat Ravine
31. Gnat Marshes
32. Munster Highlands
33. Mousehara Desert
34. Oasis of the Sweaty Camel
35. Cabbagehead Hill
36. Rattytrap Jungle
37. Rio Mosquito

Dear mouse friends,
Thanks for reading, and farewell
till the next book.
It'll be another whisker-licking-good
adventure, and that's a promise!

Geronimo Stilton